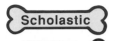

Clifford THE BIG RED DOG®

The Windy Day

by Sonali Fry
Illustrated by the Thompson Bros.

Cartwheel
·B·O·O·K·S·®

SCHOLASTIC INC.
New York   Toronto   London   Auckland   Sydney
Mexico City   New Delhi   Hong Kong   Buenos Aires

Hi! I'm Emily Elizabeth, and this is
Clifford, my Big Red Dog.
Clifford always tries his best
to make me happy.

One day, I was painting a picture
of Clifford in Birdwell Island Park.

I was almost finished when the wind blew my painting up and away!

Clifford ran after it....

But he didn't see Mr. Bleakman,
who was feeding some squirrels.

Then Clifford saw my painting drift toward Sheriff Lewis. So Clifford followed it.

Sheriff Lewis was eating a yummy cupcake.

But when Clifford went running through…

T-Bone got to taste some, too!

When my painting flew toward the playground, Clifford finally caught it!
He was so excited that he didn't see Jetta.

Again, Clifford was very sorry.

I was happy to get my painting back.

But everyone else was mad!

Clifford didn't mean to cause trouble.

He just wanted to get my painting for me.

I took Clifford to the pier, where Charley was selling lemonade.

Suddenly it got very, very windy.

Everyone gathered on the pier.

"What's going on?" we wondered.

Then we looked toward the sea: It was a tornado!

And it was heading toward Birdwell Island!

"What are we going to do?" we cried.

We were all scared.

Except for Clifford, that is.

My big, brave red dog swam out
into the sea.

He took a deep breath…

and blew the tornado far, far away.

Birdwell Island was safe!

Clifford may have caused
a little trouble that day,
but in the end he was a hero.
Hooray for Clifford!